The Midnight Pig

W9-BGJ-637

For Miriam Krueger

Contents

Chapter 1

We called Fred the "Midnight Pig" because that's when he usually ate. We owned the local store, and by the time Mom had closed up and prepared for the next day, it was usually about midnight. The old clock would strike twelve, play a tune, and Mom would throw out cabbage leaves, vegetable peels, and any other leftover food. Fred would wolf it down.

I can still remember the day I got Fred. It was my first day at my new school. We had just moved from the city. It was all Mom's idea. When my parents split up, the house was sold and Mom bought an old store. It was way out in the country. The total population of the whole town was only 800. Well, I guess it's 804 now.

When the moving van pulled up outside the store, I thought we were just stopping to buy something.

"Well, what do you think?" Mom asked.

Mark and Peter stared at me, their eyes wide. No one said anything for a while.

"I know it needs some work," Mom said, "but just think, our own home and business!"

"But, Mom!" Mark roared, "none of my friends will ever visit me here. The doorway might fall down on top of them."

"I want to go home," Peter bawled.

"Don't be silly," Mom said. She wasn't going to listen to any more complaining, and she quickly had us dragging all our belongings up the rickety, old stairs. To make things worse, the bottom part of the banister dissolved into a pile of dust as I touched it.

It wasn't only our house that was run-down. Our new school looked like an old farm building. Ms. Sharp, my new teacher, was tall and thin with a huge mop of bushy hair. She looked like a broom with glasses. Unfortunately, I had to sit next to Lizzie Bean, the meanest girl in the whole school. For some reason, she didn't like me right from the start.

"Hey, Chicken Legs, keep your elbow to yourself!" she said as we were writing. She purposely knocked against my arm.

"Ouch," I cried.

"Kylie, please work quietly," Ms. Sharp said as she looked up from her grading.

I moved as far away as I could, but Lizzie wouldn't give up. She thumped her elbow into me again, this time much harder. I let out a yell.

"Kylie, come here a moment, please," Ms. Sharp said. She obviously knew what Lizzie was like and was feeling sorry for me. "Kylie, I know you just moved here, and making new friends can be hard. My brother has ten piglets on his farm that he's wanting to find homes for. I wonder if you would like to have one? Perhaps you could ask your mother."

Although Mom was hesitant at first, she finally agreed to me having a pet pig. That evening, Fred arrived. When I heard the knock on the door, I raced my brothers to answer it. A big man with suntanned skin stood at the door with a small, pink bundle in his arms.

"It's a pig!" Mark said excitedly.

"Can I have it?" Peter asked, wide-eyed.

"It's for Kylie," the man said.

The next thing I knew, I was holding Fred in my arms.

Mom still wasn't sure about us having a pet pig. "But, we don't need a pig," she said.

"Please, Mom," Mark and Peter pleaded. "It would make living here a lot better."

I could see that he had pressed the right button. "Oh, all right," she said reluctantly.

"Can I make a bed for him?" Mark asked.

"You can use one of the vegetable crates," Mom said, "and put an old cushion in it."

In about ten seconds flat, Mark came rushing back with Fred's new bed. He'd put one of Mom's pink bedroom cushions in the bottom of the crate. Mom nearly had a fit.

"That's my cushion!" she spluttered.

"But, Mom, it's pink; it color-coordinates with Fred," I argued.

Mom was quiet, and I could see she was thinking. "It might be a boy pig," she said.

She looked at Fred and said, "Yes, he definitely is a boy. Pink is not for boys."

"Oh, don't be so old-fashioned, Mom. Fred won't mind," Peter said. As it turned out, Fred didn't mind at all. He loved his new pink cushion. He snuggled into its quilted softness, making little snuffling noises. Mom just shook her head and changed the subject.

"So, what's his name going to be?" she asked.

"How about Peter?" Peter said.

"Don't be silly," Mark said. "You and the pig can't have the same name. Why don't we call him Hercules?"

"He's my pig, and I want to call him Fred," I said.

"That's a good name," Mom said.

So, Fred it was. He slept in his bed in the kitchen until he was old enough to sleep outside. That's when Mom started feeding him at midnight. It became a habit, like brushing our teeth after the six-o'clock news.

Fred wasn't always predictable. He certainly could get himself into a lot of mischief.

The worst thing he ever did was climb onto Mom's bed and snuggle her soft, pink quilt with his thoroughly muddy body.

When Mom saw him, she hit the roof. "Get that pig off my bed!" she yelled. Fred didn't seem to understand what all the fuss was about. As it turned out, Mom used up a whole can of air freshener in her room, and she spent a long time trying to wash the mud out of her quilt.

"That pig is an absolute, total nuisance!" I overheard her saying to one of her customers.

"You should sell him to Brian Murdoch," the customer said as he was leaving. "He always buys a pig for the holidays."

I stood at the door, looking at Mom. I could picture the wheels turning in her head. My blood froze. "Mom, you wouldn't ever do that, would you?" I asked.

She grunted something and turned to admire Mrs. Stephens's new baby. At the same time, a man entered the store. He was about thirty, tall and thin, and dressed mainly in black. His brown hair coiled into tiny, tight curls.

He stood in the shadow by the front door, watching Mom talk to Mrs. Stephens. His eyes were riveted on the open cash register. He didn't say or do anything, but something about him made me shiver.

Chapter 2

As time went by, things started to settle down, and I became quite happy in our new town. Fred, however, had a habit of making life difficult for me. I got a part in the school play, so I went to rehearsal after school. The play went really well – sort of. We performed it at the Town Hall, in front of all the parents. The only thing that ruined it was Fred.

He must have followed Mom to the Town Hall and stood, watching through the open doorway. In the final scene, I had to collapse to the floor. Fred was obviously concerned. He clip-clopped across the floor and onto the stage. He kept grunting and butting my face with his wet nose. Everyone laughed and applauded. Mark had to pull him off the stage. Boy, was I embarrassed!

Fred was not only a loyal friend to me, he was also an excellent judge of character.

He didn't like Lizzie Bean, and he didn't like the new sales assistant Mom hired after suffering through another cold dinner.

We were eating our dinner with the door open so we would be able to hear if anyone came into the store. I had just stuffed half a sausage into my mouth when the store bell rang. Mom ran out to serve the customer. By the time she got back, her dinner was cold.

"I wish, just for once, that I could sit down to a meal and finish it without being interrupted," she began, and then she brightened. "I know, I'll hire a part-time assistant."

"What's that?" Peter asked.

"A person who comes in here and works," Mark said impatiently.

"You don't need an assistant, Mom; you've got us," I said.

"But that's exactly why I need an assistant, so we can sit down and have a meal in peace."

"But won't that cost money?" Mark asked.

"Yes," Mom said, "we'll have to do without some things, but it'll be worth it."

We soon found out that one of the things we were going to do without was having the TV repaired. This upset Fred more than it did us. He loved that TV. When it was still working, he would walk right up to the screen and snort happily. Then he would sit on his favorite pink cushion and fall asleep. Sometimes, he would snore so loudly we'd have to turn up the volume. When the TV stopped working, Fred continued to sit in front of it, with half-closed eyes, hoping it would come on.

"When's the new person coming?" I asked Mom after I'd watched poor Fred sit hopefully in front of the broken TV for half an hour.

"Today, at 4:30," she replied.

Just before 4:30, the store bell rang, and our new assistant walked in. It was the same man who had been staring at the money in the cash register. He still gave me the creeps.

"This is Tony Thompson," Mom said.

The man looked at us and smiled. His eyeteeth were longer than the rest of his teeth, making him look a bit like a cat. That didn't bother me.

But for some reason I couldn't quite put my finger on, I just didn't trust him.

"Just call me Tony," he said, smiling broadly.

"Well, kids, Tony is going to work for us from 4:30 until closing time. It'll sure make life a lot easier," Mom said. She showed Tony where we kept everything and how to work the register. His eyes seemed to be drawn to the neatly stacked piles of money.

"You'll learn quickly," Mom assured him.

"Oh, I'm sure I will, Mrs. Henderson," he said.

"Please, call me Cheryl," Mom laughed.

Then the two of them went out back to check the stock.

"He's cool," Mark said.

I glared at him. "No, he's not," I said firmly.

"What's wrong with him?" Peter asked.

"I don't quite know," I said. "Maybe it's the way he seems to stare at the money in the cash register." The boys just shrugged.

As soon as Mom and Tony got back, Fred came in from outside to see who was there. He always liked to know who was in the store.

Even when he was sitting by the TV, he would open one eye when the bell rang. If he recognized the voice, he would close his eye again. This time, he just walked up to Tony and grunted.

"What a cute little pig," Tony said, reaching out a hand to pet Fred. To everyone's surprise, Fred snorted loudly and started grunting.

"Stop it, Fred!" Mom shouted.

"Yeah, Fred, you're not being very sociable," Peter said proudly. "Sociable" was his new word for the week.

Fred just kept on snorting and grunting. I was embarrassed and took him out back. When he saw his cushion, he settled down.

"I don't like Tony Thompson, either," I whispered into Fred's hairy ear. As it turned out, my suspicions about Tony were right.

Chapter 3

At assembly on Monday, Mr. Davis made an announcement. "We are going to hold a garden contest to celebrate horticulture week."

"What's that?" Peter asked Michael Johnson.

"Gardening week," Michael whispered.

"Because there are four garden areas, we will divide the school into four groups," Mr. Davis continued. "I have chosen the group leaders. Would the following children please come to the front: Lizzie Bean, Leroy Jones, Martin Jackson, and Kylie Henderson."

I turned bright red. I could feel everyone staring at me as I shuffled to the front.

"Now, we will quietly form into our groups and spend the morning preparing the gardens," Mr. Davis finished with an encouraging smile.

I was glad Mark was in my group, and I got him to help me get our tools out of the shed.

Lizzie Bean's group had already started. She was really enjoying herself, yelling out directions while the others worked.

"Look at them; they really dig gardening!" Mark said, laughing at his own joke.

"This is a great area for a garden," I said as we came to our patch. But the moment I started digging, I heard a snuffling behind me. Fred had come to see what we were doing. He was so excited, he couldn't stop snorting.

"Kylie, you can't have Fred here!" Ms. Sharp said, shooing him away from the garden. "No pigs allowed." Fred stayed at the side, looking longingly at the newly turned dirt.

"The plants are on the porch," Mr. Davis announced loudly. "The teachers will divide them among the groups."

We spent the next hour planting and watering the seedlings. I could see Fred waiting patiently in the distance. He had one eye on Ms. Sharp and the other on the gardens. When we had finished, we all stood back to admire our work.

"I bet you that we'll win, Chicken Legs," Lizzie Bean said as she walked toward me.

"You can't win everything!" I said angrily.

"Do you want to bet?" Lizzie asked as she pushed me. It wasn't a hard push, not hard enough for anyone to notice. But it was enough to make me lose my balance and fall right on top of my group's garden.

"Yuck!" I said as I felt my muddy hair.

"Kylie fell down," Peter shouted.

"Oh, Kylie, please try to be careful," Ms. Sharp said, pulling me up. "You'll have to go inside and get cleaned up."

"Chicken Legs really did it this time," Lizzie Bean said, laughing.

Now I was completely embarrassed. I was covered in mud, and everyone was staring at me. I had to take a shower, and the school gave me some clothes that didn't quite fit.

Ms. Sharp handed me a plastic bag with my muddy clothes inside. "Another job for the washing machine," she said. I didn't tell her that our machine was broken.

By three o'clock, I was glad to be going home. As I was picking up my bag, I heard a loud yell.

"Look at what that pig's done!"

Everyone rushed outside. There was Fred, happily rolling around in the middle of Lizzie Bean's garden. He was covered in mud and squashed seedlings.

"My garden's ruined!" Lizzie shouted.

"Oh, well, I don't think your garden will win the contest now," Martin Jackson said with a smirk on his face.

I didn't hear the end of it for ages. Mr. Davis bought some new plants with money from the swimming-pool fund. None of Lizzie's group would even speak to me, especially after my garden won the contest. That was bad, but nothing compared to what happened next.

Mom called us into the kitchen. She had a long face and was drumming her fingers uneasily on the table.

"We have a problem," she said. "We're having financial difficulty."

"What's that?" Peter asked.

"It means we're broke," Mark said.

"Well, not exactly broke. But we are behind with the store payments," Mom admitted.

"But I thought we bought the store, Mom," I said.

"Well, we did, but with a loan from the bank," Mom continued. "Now they're demanding that I immediately pay what I owe them or we'll lose the store."

None of us could think of anything to say.

"I think I may have found a way to make the payment. I've got some money saved up, but not enough." Mom hesitated before continuing. "I could do it if we sold Fred."

After a short period of silence, the bomb hit. "What?" the three of us roared. Mom explained that Brian Murdoch was willing to give her a good price for Fred.

"But something awful might happen to him! Please, Mom. I'll never get over it. You just can't sell Fred." The tears were streaming down my cheeks. Mom put her arm around me.

"Kylie, it's not that bad," she said. "Mr. Murdoch only wants him for breeding. As soon as we're on our feet again, we'll buy Fred back.

That made me feel a little better, but I made her promise that as soon as we had the money, Fred would be ours again.

It was the saddest day of my life. I took Fred up the hill, to Mr. Murdoch's farm. Mark and Peter slowly followed behind me. Fred thought he was just going for a walk and trotted happily beside me, snuffling as he went.

Lizzie Bean came around the corner and asked me where I was going with Fred.

"To Mr. Murdoch's farm," I said, trying not to let her see my tears.

"Mr. Murdoch? He buys a pig every year for the holidays," she reminded me.

I knew Mom had promised that nothing bad would happen, but Lizzie's comment made my blood freeze. I felt glued to the ground and wished it would just swallow me up. As it turned out, it was Mr. Murdoch who came to the rescue.

"Hello, Kylie," he said. "I see you've brought the pig. My, he's a beauty!"

I stared at him through my tears. Mr. Murdoch was a big man with a stubbly white beard. "Come this way," he said, smiling at me.

I was crying so much, I had trouble seeing where I was going.

"Now, pig," Mr. Murdoch said as he stopped and patted Fred. "You're worth a nice price, I'll bet. Thank you, Kylie," Mr. Murdoch said as he handed me some money.

I didn't even count it. I just started walking slowly down the hill. I was so upset, I nearly didn't hear Mr. Murdoch call out.

"Kylie, I wonder if you and your brothers could do me a big favor," he asked.

I stopped and slowly turned around. I was crying so much, I could taste the tears trickling into my mouth.

"I was wondering if you could look after my new pig for me," he asked.

I didn't know what he meant. "What new pig?" I answered, finally finding my voice.

"Why, this beautiful pig here," he laughed, pointing to Fred.

I just stared at Mr. Murdoch. He was grinning. I knew right then that I liked him, and I understood what he was doing. He was giving Fred back to me. I rushed up and threw my arms around him.

"Oh, thank you, Mr. Murdoch," I said in a quiet voice.

"Hey, you're doing me a favor," he said. "I don't have enough room here for another pig."

I knew he really did have enough room and was just being kind. I felt so happy, I wanted to dance. We came back down that hill so quickly, we almost flew. Mom says pigs can't fly. Well, Fred nearly did. When we got back, he trotted through the shop, past Mrs. Stephens and her new baby, past Mom with her mouth open wide, and plonked himself down on his cushion.

"What's that pig doing back here?" Mom asked suspiciously.

"Mr. Murdoch wanted us to look after him."

"Oh, come on, Kylie," Mom said. "Why would he do that? You didn't even take Fred to the farm, did you?"

"Yes, of course I did. Look, here's the money to prove it." I proudly handed her the wad of money.

Mom looked pretty confused as she counted all of the money and stared at Fred.

She was about to comment, when the store bell rang. Instead, she disappeared into the store.

"Oh, Mr. Murdoch," I heard her say. We all raced after her. I was panicking. Maybe he changed his mind.

"Hello, kids," he said, still smiling. "I've just come to make sure that my pig is OK."

I sighed with relief. "He's watching the broken TV," Peter said.

Mr. Murdoch laughed. "Oh, is he? Well then, maybe he'd like a TV dinner." He went outside and was quickly back with a bucket of slop, Fred's favorite food.

"But he always eats his slop at midnight," Peter said. "That's why we call him the 'Midnight Pig.'"

"Well, I don't think I can stay that late. It's a good thing you're looking after him," replied Mr. Murdoch, noticing the puzzled look on Mom's face. "I did buy the pig, and I appointed these three children as his guardians."

"What's a guardian?" Peter asked.

"Someone to look after him," Mark said.

Mom suddenly got it. She smiled, then she started laughing. Finally, she shook hands with Mr. Murdoch. "Thank you so much," she said. "I guess I really like that pig, too."

"So do I," Mr. Murdoch replied. "That's why I think he needs special attention."

"He's the best pig in the world!" Peter shouted.

Fred just slept through it all.

Chapter 4

It was good having Tony Thompson look after the store. Mom got to help us with our homework, and Tony managed to fix the TV. Still, for some reason, I didn't like him. Mom said I was being mean.

"He's had a hard life, Kylie," she said one day. "He had an accident years ago, and he's not able to work long hours. The little bit of money that we pay him really helps."

I still didn't trust him, and it didn't take long to find out why. A few days later, I was cleaning the shelves in the store and Tony was waiting on Mrs. Bean. That's when it happened. Tony handed Mrs. Bean her change, and as she was turning to go, he took a fifty-dollar bill from the cash register. He quickly closed the register and put the money in his pocket. The bell jingled as Mrs. Bean left.

Tony noticed me staring at him. "What are you looking at?" he spouted.

"I saw what you did," I said defiantly.

"What do you mean?" he asked.

"I saw you put that fifty-dollar bill in your pocket, and I'm going to tell my mom," I said. I marched past him and out the door. Before I got to Mom, I realized I needed more proof. Tony wasn't exactly going to keep the money on him. It would be my word against his. I decided right there and then that I would get that proof.

I needed time to think and decided to go for a walk. The last person I wanted to see was Lizzie, but there she was, standing by her gate.

"What's the hurry, Chicken Legs?" she called out as I walked past.

I didn't give her the satisfaction of an answer. I just increased my pace. I found a quiet spot and sat down. Suddenly, I was covered with mosquitoes. They dined on me until I couldn't stand it any longer.

"You guys are more annoying than Lizzie!" I yelled, and then I started to walk back home.

Lizzie must have been waiting for me. She was just about to insult me again, when she stepped on a bee. She jumped up and down, squealing louder than Fred does when someone tries to pick him up.

"You need to take the stinger out!" I shouted.

She must have heard me, because she threw herself onto the grass. I carefully extracted the stinger without squeezing the poison sac. "If you squeeze the sac, the poison will go into your bloodstream," I explained. "My mom told me that. She used to be a nurse. It won't hurt so much now."

Lizzie calmed down and looked me over carefully. For the first time, I noticed that she had one brown eye and one green eye.

"Thanks," she managed to mumble.

After that, she didn't call me Chicken Legs quite so often.

I still hadn't solved the problem of Tony and, as it turned out, I had a more pressing problem. Fred was sick! He lay on his cushion, sneezing and snuffling. I felt his head, and he was hot.

"Mom, Fred's sick," Mark said.

Mom looked at Fred. He stared back at her with watery eyes and then let out a huge sneeze.

"His temperature is very high," she said. "I think we'd better take him to see the vet."

Mom called the veterinarian. "He said to bring him in right away."

"Right away" took a lot longer than we had hoped. Fred put up quite a fight. When we finally arrived at the vet's, the waiting room was full. We managed to find a place to sit down.

A little boy came in with his mother and a puppy with a bandaged foot.

"Would you like to eat your lunch while we're waiting?" the boy's mother asked him.

The boy nodded, pulling out some wrapped sandwiches from a brown paper bag. Before anyone could react, Fred had wolfed down the sandwiches, paper and all.

"Mom, that pig ate my lunch!" the boy shouted and began to cry.

My mom was so embarrassed. "I'd be happy to pay for that," she said. "I really am very sorry."

"No, that's all right," the boy's mother said.

Luckily, the vet finally called out Fred's name. But Fred wasn't so full of energy then.

He took one look at him in his white coat, and sat himself back down on the floor.

"Come on, Fred. I'm not that bad," the vet said, offering him a potato. Fred was up in a flash and happily trotted into the examining room. While he was busy with the potato, the vet examined him. He pulled out his stethoscope and listened to Fred's chest. It was a wonder he could hear anything with all the noise Fred was making.

"He's got a very bad cold," the vet finally said. "I'm going to give him an injection, and then you'll need to put antibiotics in his food for a week." He brought out a syringe with a long needle.

"Oh!" Peter cried.

But Fred didn't seem to mind the injection. He sat patiently as the vet did what had to be done.

When we got back home, Mom filled a hot-water bottle and put a quilt over Fred. "You'll have to sleep inside for a while, Fred," she said.

Fred was pleased. The only thing he objected to was the medicine we put in his food. He just looked at it, grunted, put his head down on the carpet, and closed his eyes.

"Fred, you have to take your medicine," I said. But Fred wouldn't budge.

Then Peter had a brilliant idea. He suggested putting the medicine in the slop that Fred enjoyed at midnight. We all waited up to see what would happen. The clock struck twelve, and much to our relief, Fred gulped it all down.

Because of all the fuss with Fred getting sick, I had nearly forgotten about Tony. It wasn't until Fred got better that I began to focus again on what Tony was doing. One day, I wanted to use the phone when Tony was working in the store. Mom suggested I use the upstairs phone. We had just put it in, and Mom loved to say "the upstairs phone." I went upstairs and picked it up. I could hear a man's voice on the other end. I was about to put the receiver back, when I heard something that made me shiver.

"So, Friday is the day then?" the man asked.

It was Tony who answered. "Yes, we'll do it on Friday."

There was something about the tone of his voice that made my blood freeze. I didn't hang up, because I was afraid Tony would hear me. Instead, I set the receiver on the hall table.

Then I ran down the stairs. I sat outside petting Fred. He was much better now. He put his head on my knee and looked up. That's what I liked most about Fred. He made you feel as if you were the most important person in the world.

"I think Tony is up to something, Fred," I said. Fred gave a grunt of agreement.

Later, when I was sure that Tony was busy with a customer, I carefully put the receiver back on the hook.

The next day dawned bright and clear. As I tried to figure out what Tony was planning, someone called. Mom was busy and asked me to answer the phone. I sprinted up the stairs and picked up the receiver.

"Hello," I said.

"Hello, Kylie." I froze. It was Tony. "Could you tell your mother I'll be late to work today?"

"Yeah, sure," I answered.

"I've got something I have to do," he said.

I could feel a shiver traveling down my spine. Today was Tuesday. I wondered if this had anything to do with what was planned for Friday.

"Thanks, Kylie," he said before hanging up.

I just stood there, listening to the dial tone. Tony Thompson was definitely up to something, and it wasn't good. When Mom finished with a customer, I told her about the call.

"How late is he going to be?" she asked.

"He didn't say. Mom, I think Tony is up to something," I said.

"Kylie," snapped Mom, "don't be silly." I could tell by the look on her face that I shouldn't say anything else. And Tuesday was allowance day, so I didn't want to say anything that would upset her.

"Now, put this in your bank account," she reminded us as she handed us our allowance.

None of us liked saving our money. We would rather spend it. So we took a long time walking to the bank.

"Tony's going to be late today," I informed the boys as we dawdled along the sidewalk.

"He's cool," Mark said.

"No, he's not," I answered quickly. "I overheard him on the phone the other day. He said he was going to do something on Friday."

"Like what?" Peter asked.

"I don't know," I said. "But it was just the way he said it. It was like he was going to do something awful."

Mark frowned. "Maybe he's just going to do something he's always wanted to do," he said.

"Like what?" I asked.

"Oh, I don't know," Mark said, "like go out on a double date or something."

I didn't buy that. I knew Tony wasn't talking about a date. He was going to do something bad.

When we arrived at the bank, I was surprised to see Tony sitting at one of the tables, filling out a form.

"There, you see? He's probably just taking out money to buy something," Mark said.

We waited in line. When our turn finally came, Betty, the teller, smiled as she looked toward the door. "Where's Fred?"

"Asleep," Peter said. "I think he knows pigs aren't allowed in banks."

As we walked out, I noticed that Tony was still sitting at the table, writing something. He was concentrating so hard, he didn't notice us. I didn't believe Mark's explanation of what Tony was doing in the bank, and I kept thinking about it all the way home.

Later that evening, Tony arrived for work. As I dusted the shelves, I managed to keep an eye on him. The shop was quiet, with only a few customers. This didn't bother Tony. He was intently studying a piece of paper and didn't notice me watching him.

"See you tomorrow, Cheryl," he said. The store bell jingled as he left.

"OK, Tony," Mom said. "Kylie, could you unpack that box of baked beans and stack them on the shelf, please?"

I ripped open the box and started stacking the cans. As I was working, I noticed something sticking out of the trash can behind the counter. I knew what it was right when I saw it.

It was the paper Tony had been looking at all evening. I carefully lifted it out of the trash and smoothed it flat. At first, I couldn't make sense of it. It just seemed like a lot of random lines. Then I had a closer look. Suddenly, it all fit together like the pieces of a jigsaw puzzle.

I was looking at a detailed plan of the bank. Tony Thompson was going to rob the bank on Friday! I ran to tell Mom.

"Mom, Tony's going to rob the bank! Look," I said triumphantly, holding up the piece of paper.

Mom looked at it closely. "It looks like a floor plan," she said after a while.

"It's a floor plan of the bank," I said as Mark and Peter came downstairs in their pajamas to see what all the fuss was about.

"It's the bank," Mark said, looking closely at the drawing. "Look, here's the door and there's the big window."

"See," I said. "Tony's working out the exact layout of the bank so he can rob it."

"Wow," Peter said excitedly. "Will the police take him to jail?"

"Of course not," Mom said. "He hasn't done anything wrong. So what if it's a plan of the bank? It doesn't mean anything."

"I just remembered, he's taking a course in technical drawing on his night off," Mark said. "He showed me some of his designs. That drawing is just a sketch. He must be studying old buildings."

This seemed to satisfy Mom, but I just knew there was going to be trouble.

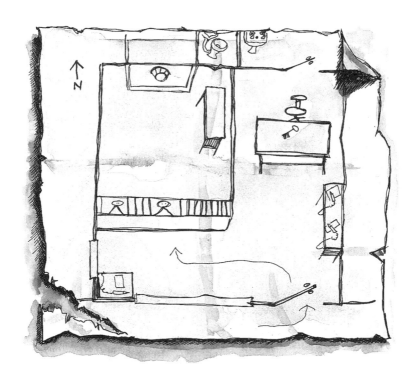

Chapter 6

The next day, we were in the kitchen when Tony popped his head around the corner. "Can I talk to you a minute, Cheryl?" he asked.

"Sure, Tony, what's up?" Mom asked.

"I have to give you my notice," he said.

I saw a look of surprise come over Mom's face. She swallowed.

"My mother is sick," continued Tony. "I need to spend some time with her. I'm sure you'll be able to get someone else."

"Well, I suppose so," Mom said rather hesitantly. "I'll put an ad in the paper. When do you have to leave?"

"Before Friday," Tony said. I choked on a piece of carrot.

"But that's the day after tomorrow," Mom said. "Aren't you supposed to give me at least two weeks' notice?"

"I know, but Mom's getting worse," Tony replied sheepishly.

Suddenly, Mom seemed to cheer up. "Oh, I just remembered. The vet's sister is looking for some part-time work."

Tony looked relieved. "Well, thanks, Cheryl. It's been good working for you."

"We'll miss you. You've done a good job here, Tony," Mom replied.

"Thanks again, Cheryl. I'll see you, kids. Bye, Fred." Tony patted Fred, who looked up and grunted loudly. Usually, everyone who came into the kitchen got plastered with a wet slobbery kiss, but not Tony. Fred just didn't like him.

My thoughts must have been written all over my face, because Mark looked over at me and said, "You look like you've just seen a ghost."

"You do look a bit pale, Kylie. Are you feeling all right?" Mom asked.

"I think it must be the casserole," Peter said hopefully as he pushed aside his half-eaten meal.

"Don't you see?" I asked.

"See what?" Mom said.

I lowered my voice, "Tony is leaving because he's going to rob the bank on Friday!"

"Oh, Kylie, you heard him. He's going to look after his mother," Mom said, obviously running out of patience.

I was getting tired of no one listening to me. "Well, he isn't exactly going to say, 'Excuse me, Cheryl, I'm giving my notice because I'm going to rob the bank on Friday.'" I was still whispering but getting really annoyed.

"Let's just drop it!" Mom said. "The bank is not going to be robbed."

But she was wrong. On Friday afternoon, at precisely 3:30, two men wearing masks held up the bank. They got away with thousands of dollars. There were police cars and tracking dogs everywhere. A helicopter kept circling over the town like a noisy bird. Even then, Mom wasn't convinced. I was beginning to think that maybe I was letting my imagination get to me.

Later that night, I was lying in bed, when I heard Fred grunting loudly. Nobody else seemed to notice. I crept downstairs. The light was still on in the store. Mom was doing the accounts.

"I'll see what Fred wants," I said as I walked past her. Then I slipped out into the darkness. Fred was snorting and grunting.

"Fred," I called softly. He looked at me and grunted again, but he wouldn't move.

I was tired. "Fred, stop making all that noise," I said. "Come here."

Fred still wouldn't budge. I was going over to get him, when I saw Tony Thompson. He was walking toward the old graveyard. I knew I shouldn't do it, but I decided to follow him.

He never saw me as I crept slowly behind him. I was really scared, but something kept urging me on. The wet grass felt cold under my bare feet. I followed him through the field and behind the gravestones. The moon was round and silvery in the black sky.

He turned suddenly, and I had just enough time to wedge myself behind a gravestone.

I waited, not daring to move. I could hear my own breathing. I listened for the slightest sound, and although I could hear nothing, I knew he was still there.

I carefully leaned forward and looked past the gravestone. He was there in the distance, a black shadow in the moonlight. I wanted to run away, but I had to find out what he was doing. He started moving again, and I followed silently. He was headed for an old, empty house.

The kids always made jokes about the house, saying it was haunted.

I watched as Tony Thompson opened the broken front door and disappeared inside. I crept slowly up to the house, trying not to make a sound. All the windows were broken. I could hear talking, and I crouched down in the long grass to listen. It was a still night, and I could hear every word.

"Good work, Tony." It was a voice I didn't recognize.

"I think we pulled it off," I heard Tony reply. "Nobody would ever look for the money here." They both laughed. "The only person who suspects a thing is one stupid kid," Tony said. "But no one will believe her."

I felt like I was going to be sick. I knew I was asking for trouble, but it was like watching a scary movie. You just had to look.

"Do you think people bought your story?" the other man asked.

"Sure," Tony said confidently. "Everyone knows my mom is sick."

"Tomorrow, we'll be a thousand miles away," Tony's partner said.

"Yeah, I'll go up and see my mom tomorrow before we leave. Nobody will think I had anything to do with the robbery. I'll come back and visit her from time to time. I can certainly afford to travel," Tony laughed.

My legs were starting to ache, and I had to move them. Something underneath me snapped. It was only a small noise, but I knew they heard it. I ran across the grass, terrified. I didn't see the broken gravestone until it was too late. I went flying head over heels. Before I knew it, wet, clammy hands were clutching my shoulders. Tony Thompson looked down at me, smiling. His eyes were glazed.

"Look what we have here," he said breathlessly. "This is the little brat I was telling you about."

Chapter 7

He dragged me into the old house. It was dark, but I could see his grinning face.

"Now, what will we do with you?" he said.

I couldn't speak. I was so frightened, I was having trouble breathing. Just when I thought there was no hope, I heard a man's voice outside the house.

"Police," the voice boomed.

Tony let go of me, grabbed the suitcase, and rushed out into the night. The other man just stood there, not knowing what to do. The police officers grabbed him while tracking dogs chased Tony through the graveyard. The suitcase fell open, and money fluttered in the wind like confetti. One of the dogs latched onto Tony's arm, and Tony was quickly handcuffed.

"Are you all right, Kylie?" a police officer asked as she put an arm around my shoulders.

I just cried onto her jacket. "It's all right, Kylie," she said. "Everything's going to be fine. You've done us a great favor, you and your pig."

Two of the officers took me home. When I got there, Fred was all over me, slobbering and snuffling. He seemed very happy to see me.

"How did you find me? How did you know I was there?" I asked the officers after Fred had finally flopped down beside me.

"We didn't find you; it's your pig you've got to thank for that!" one officer said. "We should have tracking pigs on the force." Then everyone laughed.

"But what did Fred do?" I asked.

Before the officer could answer, Mom did something that surprised everyone. She gave Fred a kiss right on his wet, sloppy snout.

"Yuck!" exclaimed Mark. Everyone burst out laughing again.

"Fred is a pig in a million," Mom said. "If it weren't for him, well, who knows what might have happened."

"Yes, but what did happen?" I asked eagerly.

"Well, at midnight, I went to find Fred," Mom said. "He wasn't here. I looked everywhere, and I couldn't find him. It was really puzzling, and I thought maybe he was in your room. I went upstairs and, of course, you weren't there. I looked outside. I looked everywhere, and then I called the police."

"That's when we figured it out," the other police officer said, continuing the story. "We discovered that Tony Thompson's mother had taken a turn for the worse yesterday, and was asking for her son. Nobody could find him, and then it all made sense. We were worried that you may have tried to catch the robbers by yourself."

"Then we saw Fred," Mom said. "He was standing by the fence, making a lot of noise, and his feet were muddy. He stood there looking panicked, and just wouldn't stop squealing."

"So we followed him," the officer continued. "He led us right to you."

I stared at Fred. He had his head on my blanket and was snoring. "But how did he know where I was?" I asked, still a little confused.

"Well, he obviously followed you," Mom said. "He knew exactly where you were."

"But I didn't see him," I said.

"What's important is that he saw you," Mom said with a smile.

So that was it. Tony and the other man were arrested. The money was taken back to the bank, and Fred and I got our photo in the paper. Fred didn't enjoy having his photo taken. He was more interested in trying to eat the camera.

That evening, a special present arrived for Fred. It came in a police car, and the officers who took me home delivered it personally. It was a big, blue bucket of slop with a pink ribbon. Fred not only ate the slop, he ate the ribbon, too.

Since then, not much has happened. Fred has gotten a lot fatter, and Lizzie Bean has gotten a lot nicer. We are really much happier now.

So is Fred!

From the Author

 My grandfather had a pet pig when he was a boy. I grew up hearing about all the wonderful things that this pig had done. I also remember hearing about how my grandfather and his brothers had to take the pig to the butcher. The pig never came home again. I decided to write a story about a pig that did make it back home.

A while ago, my husband was a star witness in a court case. He actually saw a man drawing a sketch of the floor plan inside a bank. After the bank was robbed, my husband told the police what he had seen, and the police found the sketch inside the man's house. I thought that this would make a good story.

I have had twenty-five books published, but *The Midnight Pig* is my favorite.

Carol Krueger

From the Illustrator

 I've always loved drawing and feel very fortunate to earn my living doing something I enjoy. For most of the year, I design and animate cartoons for TV. And believe me, there's plenty of drawing involved (up to twenty-five images for one second of movement).

Whenever I need a change, there's nothing I like more than illustrating a good book. When I read *The Midnight Pig*, I was hooked. It has everything I enjoy most: great characters, an excellent adventure, and a pig with personality!

John Bennett

Written by **Carol Krueger**
Illustrated by **John Bennett**
Edited by **Frances Bacon**
Designed by **Kristie Rogers**

© 1997 Shortland Publications Inc.
All rights reserved.

04 03 02 01 00
10 9 8 7 6 5 4 3

Distributed in the United States of America by
Rigby
a division of Reed Elsevier Inc.
P.O. Box 797
Crystal Lake, IL 60039-0797

Printed by Colorcraft, Hong Kong
ISBN: 0-7901-1664-2